Skunkdog

Emily Jenkins　　Pictures by **Pierre Pratt**

Frances Foster Books / Farrar, Straus and Giroux / New York

To Frances Foster, in thanks for her
ongoing support of my work
—E.J.

To Louca Corôa and her Corôas
—P.P.

Text copyright © 2008 by Emily Jenkins
Pictures copyright © 2008 by Pierre Pratt
All rights reserved
Distributed in Canada by Douglas & McIntyre Ltd.
Color separations by Chroma Graphics PTE Ltd.
Printed and bound in the United States of America by Worzalla
Designed by Jay Colvin
First edition, 2008
1 3 5 7 9 10 8 6 4 2

www.fsgkidsbooks.com

Library of Congress Cataloging-in-Publication Data
Jenkins, Emily, date.
    Skunkdog / Emily Jenkins ; pictures by Pierre Pratt.— 1st ed.
        p.   cm.
    Summary: Dumpling, a lonely dog with no sense of smell, moves with her family to the
country and makes a new friend who takes some getting used to.
    ISBN-13: 978-0-374-37009-1
    ISBN-10: 0-374-37009-5
    [1. Friendship—Fiction.   2. Dogs—Fiction.   3. Skunks—Fiction.]   I. Pratt, Pierre, ill.
II. Title.

PZ7.J4134 Sku 2008
[E]—dc22
                                                                    2005054701

Dumpling was a dog of enormous enthusiasm, excellent obedience skills—and very little nose.

She was smart, too. She sat when people told her to sit, stayed when people told her to stay, and rolled over when they told her to roll over. She understood quite a lot of English and a little Spanish. She could even do tricks—though most of the time she preferred to lie down and chew on something made of rawhide.

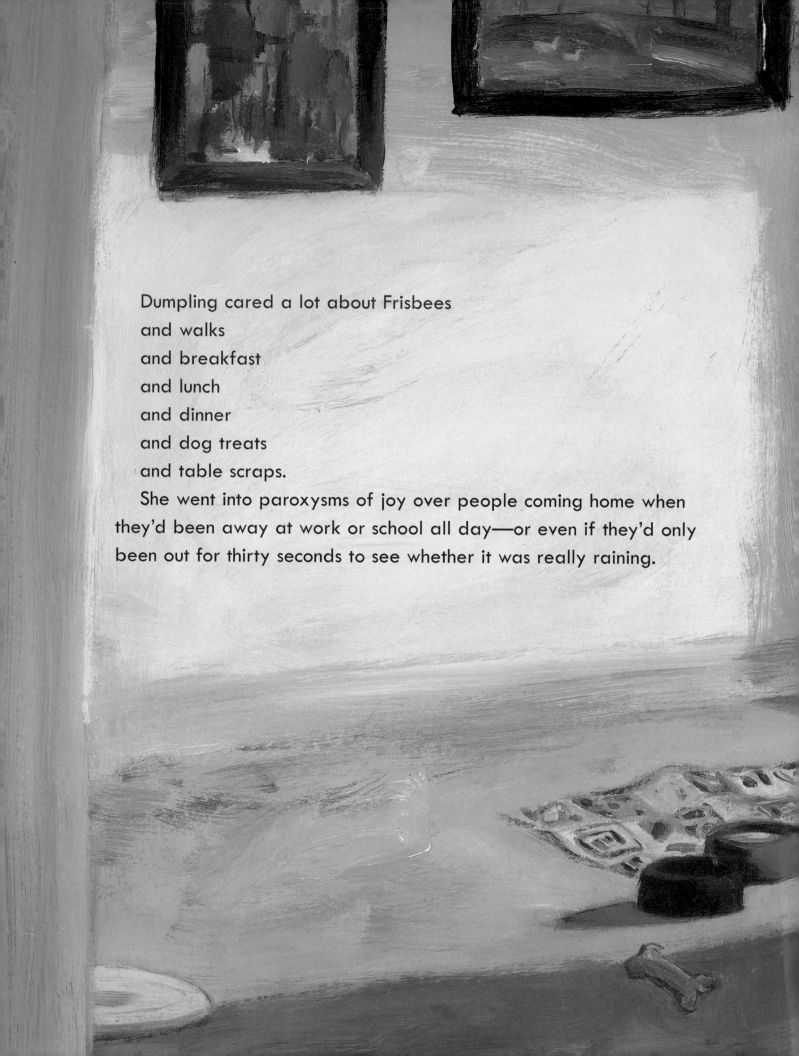

Dumpling cared a lot about Frisbees
and walks
and breakfast
and lunch
and dinner
and dog treats
and table scraps.

She went into paroxysms of joy over people coming home when they'd been away at work or school all day—or even if they'd only been out for thirty seconds to see whether it was really raining.

But unlike most dogs, who can smell a cat or a butcher shop from blocks away, Dumpling couldn't smell a thing. She didn't care about flowers, or garbage, or any of the other smelly items most dogs enjoy. And the way other dogs went sniffing around one another (you know the way they do) meant nothing at all to her.

She didn't understand what they were up to. She couldn't smell anything, so she didn't care.

As a result, Dumpling had no dog friends. None. Without a sense of smell, she couldn't relate. She loved her people, of course, and in particular the small boy who gave her table scraps and dog treats and threw the Frisbee. But she had no companions of her own species, or any other species besides human.

And so, rather often, Dumpling was lonely.

One summer day, Dumpling and her people piled into a moving van with a whole lot of furniture and boxes and took a long ride out to the country. Dumpling threw up twice on the journey and had to wear a leash when they got out at rest stops, but when they arrived at the new house, she felt it was all worthwhile. There was a large meadow nearby, a garden waiting to be planted, and long paths through the woods in the back that were perfect for walks.

Best of all, there was a doghouse just for Dumpling. The boy put her food and water dishes just outside its door, and her favorite afghan inside for a bed.

As the people finished hauling boxes from the van and the sun began to set, Dumpling explored. Next to the doghouse was an interesting bush. Dumpling was just beginning to dig an experimental hole underneath it when she caught sight of a small black-and-white creature lurking behind the foliage.

It sprayed her with some oily wet stuff—oh, my goodness!—but
Dumpling wagged her tail, to show that she was up for some fun.
The creature sprayed again, then disappeared into the woods.
Dumpling was disappointed and trotted indoors.

"Dumpling!" the people cried as soon as they smelled her. "What have you gotten into?"

"I think it's a skunk," said the mother.

"Oh, drat. We'll have to wash her right away," sighed the father. "I'll find the dog shampoo."

"Dumpling! Skunks are yucky," explained the boy. "Stay away from skunks."

The boy dragged Dumpling to the bathroom, where they all three lifted her into the tub and scrubbed her with warm water and a lot of suds.

"It's not working," said the boy.

"She still smells," said the father.

"I read somewhere that tangerine juice works to get a skunk smell out," said the mother, grabbing her wallet and heading into town.

When the mother returned with a bag of tangerines, the people sliced them in half and squeezed them all over Dumpling. Then they rinsed her and dried her off with a towel.

"It's not working," said the boy.

"She still smells," said the father.

"We have to roll her in sand, that's it," said the mother. "The sand absorbs the oil in the skunk spray."

She picked up Dumpling, still wrapped in the towel. They all got in the car and drove to the lake.

"Roll over!" the boy said to Dumpling. And because she was an obedient dog and always did what people told her to do, Dumpling rolled in the sand.

When she was good and sandy, they drove Dumpling home and gave her another bath.

"It's not working," said the boy.

"She still smells," said the father.

"Tomato juice," said the mother, grabbing her wallet and heading back to town.

Dumpling went back outside in search of the skunk. She couldn't smell anything, so she didn't care.

It was back under the bush, looking for something to eat.
"Woof," breathed Dumpling, softly so she wouldn't scare it.
The skunk sprayed her again. Oh, my goodness!
But Dumpling stayed put. She lowered herself onto her belly and slowly inched forward, thumping her tail.
Now, this skunk was a particularly brave animal. It could have disappeared back into the woods. But it didn't.

It stood there, looking at Dumpling. And Dumpling looked at it.
Then the skunk waddled over to Dumpling's dish, which was right next to the doghouse. It took a piece of kibble between its paws. Dumpling watched as it ate the kibble very neatly and then took another piece.
Soon they were having dinner together, Dumpling and the skunk, watching the last of the sunset through the trees.

Just then, the mother came back from town, carrying two large cans of tomato juice. "Oh no!" she moaned when she saw the two of them together. "Naughty dog! Don't play with a skunk! Yucky, stinky skunk!"

She grabbed Dumpling's collar and dragged her back into the house to the bathroom. "She got sprayed *again*!" she called to the father and the small boy. "This tomato stuff better work!"

So they washed Dumpling three more times in the bathtub. Twice with tomato juice, and then again with dog shampoo.

"It's working!" cried the boy.
"I think she smells okay," said the father.
"Finally," sighed the mother.

As soon as Dumpling was dry, the people let her outside again. "Now, Dumpling," said the small boy, "you can sleep in the doghouse. You can play in the meadow. You can chase the butterflies. But whatever you do, don't play with that yucky, stinky skunk."

As I told you before, Dumpling was a very obedient dog. She sat when people told her to sit, stayed when people told her to stay, and rolled over when they told her to roll over. But this time, she wasn't going to do as she was told.

The skunk was her friend. She had never had a friend, and now that she had one, she wasn't giving it up.

Right away, she started to look for that skunk. She looked under the bush. She went a little ways into the woods. She looked in the garden that was waiting to be planted, and underneath the porch.

The skunk was nowhere to be found.

Maybe it didn't want to be friends after all?

Maybe it didn't like when the people said "yucky, stinky skunk." Maybe its feelings were hurt.

Dumpling searched and searched for the skunk, but the only creatures she found were a couple of white butterflies and a field mouse that didn't seem very friendly.

When the people finished dinner, the boy came out with some table
scraps.

Dumpling didn't move.

The boy pulled a dog treat out of his pocket.

Dumpling didn't move.

The boy threw a Frisbee.

Dumpling didn't move.

"All right," the boy finally said, filling her water bowl and giving her some more kibble. "It'll be nice and warm in the doghouse, with your afghan. See you in the morning."

With her head hanging low, and feeling lonelier than she ever had when she lived in the city, Dumpling wagged her tail gently at him and headed in.

There in the doghouse, cuddled up on Dumpling's favorite afghan, was the skunk!

It rolled over to make room for Dumpling. The two of them lay there for a while, then spent the rest of the night romping around the meadow, stopping now and then to eat a little kibble.

From then on, Dumpling and the skunk were the best of friends. They played chase, and roll-in-the-dust, and catch-the-butterfly. They dug things out of the garden and tramped through the woods. When they got tired, they lay in the doghouse together, side by side.

And though she sometimes got sprayed, when the skunk was startled
or in a cranky mood, Dumpling never minded a bit. She couldn't smell
anything, so she didn't care.

And the people? They bought a lot of tomato juice, and kept the cans in a cupboard beneath the bathroom sink.